LITTLE RICKY
and the
DRIVING
LETTERS

WRITTEN BY
TERRI ASHCHI

Mrs. Rose was teaching her students how to write their letters. She explained that letters need to be written nicely between the lines on the writing paper.

"But writing is hard for me," thought Little Ricky. "Why does Mrs. Rose insist that I write the letters between the lines perfectly anyway?"

Just as Little Ricky was tracing his name on his paper, he felt his eyelids getting heavier and heavier and heavier as he drifted off into a deep sleep.

"Hello! I am Mimi, but you can call me Em," said Em.

"Hi, Em. My name is Little Ricky," he said. Little Ricky looked around. "Where are we?" he asked.

""We are on Alphabet Road. It is where all the letters hang out and drive," said Em.

"What? Letters drive?" asked Little Ricky in disbelief.

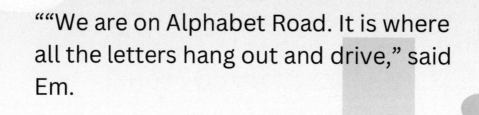

Em explained, "Have you noticed how letters in an alphabet strip are on different lines? They are on two solid lines with a dotted line in the middle. It is really a road. Just like the road your mom and dad drive on."

abcdefghijklmnopqrstuvwxyz

"Letters are famous for driving. You can see us in classrooms all over the world. Do you have an alphabet strip in your classroom, Little Ricky?" asked Em.

"Sure, we do!" said Little Ricky.

"Well, during the day, we sit nicely on our alphabet strip on the wall. After school, we do what we love to do- we drive," said Em.

Em wanted Little Ricky to meet her friends. Em pulled over to a group of letters on the side of the road.

"Little Ricky, meet my friends a, c, e, i, m, n, o, r, s, u, v, w, x, and z. We all belong to the Safe Drivers Club," Em said.

**Meet the
Safe Drivers!**

Why do they call you Safe Drivers?"
asked Little Ricky.

"Because we have a very important
rule. We stay in our lanes when we are
driving. We always drive between the
middle-dotted line and the bottom line
of the road," explained Em.

Safe Drivers
ALWAYS STAY
in their lanes!

"When you write us on your paper, always start at the dotted line and come down and touch the bottom line on your paper, but be careful not to go past the line."

"Your handwriting will look great if you do. If you want to belong to the Safe Drivers Club, you must follow our rules and stay in your lane," Em said.

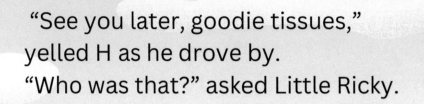

"See you later, goodie tissues," yelled H as he drove by.
"Who was that?" asked Little Ricky.

"Oh, that was H. He belongs to the Road Hog Club. We call them Road Hogs because they hog the entire road when they drive," said Em.

Meet the Road Hog Drivers!

"The letters b, d, f, h, k, l, and t all belong to the Road Hog Club. If you want to be in their club, the rule is to take up the whole road when you drive.

I guess they never heard of the phrase 'Sharing is Caring.'"

Ricky had a puzzled look on his face. "What's wrong?" asked Em. "Well, sometimes I see letters like a and c take up the whole road. I thought they were safe drivers," said Ricky.

t

"Sometimes other letters come to visit the Road Hog Club. Every letter can be a Road Hog if it is a capital letter. They are just visiting, and they are not staying, so they go back to their driving clubs.

Does that make sense?" asked Em. Little Ricky nodded his head enthusiastically.

When you write them on your paper, start at the top line and go all the way down with your pencil to the bottom line and stop," explained Em.

Just then, Letter Y drove by, and he almost crashed into them.

"Hey, watch out! That letter is driving off the road," cried Little Ricky.

"They begin driving well at the dotted line, but then they get all silly and drive right out of their lane. They go off the road all the time!"

"When you write a silly letter, just remember to start at the dotted line and then come down to the bottom line and keep writing right past it."

"If you want to belong to the Silly Drivers Club, there is one rule to follow. Just be silly! The letters g, j, p, q, and y all belong to that club," said Em.

Just be silly!

"Well, Ricky, you have just learned all about the driving clubs. You get to choose which club you would like to belong to," said Em.

"Just remember that you must follow their club rule to belong to their club," Em reminded him.

Little Ricky thought for a while. He could belong to any of the clubs because his name had Safe Drivers, Road Hogs, and Silly Drivers. He made his choice, and, just as he was about to tell Em, he heard a voice, "Little Ricky, Little Ricky!"

"Little Ricky, it's time to wake up. We are going to lunch," said Mrs. Rose. Little Ricky woke up.

Mrs. Rose looked at his paper. All his letters were neatly written between the lines, just as she had taught him.

Little Ricky closed his notebook and picked it up to put it away, and under it, he saw a card. It was a driver's license.

Little Ricky felt proud of his writing, too. He was ready to write at school and drive in his dreams with his friend Em.

About the Author

Terri Ashchi has spent most of her life teaching children how to read and write. She is passionate about helping her students succeed in school. As a teacher, she incorporates stories, songs, and movement into the learning environment. One day, while trying to teach her students how to write correctly, she created a story to teach children letter formation. She decided to write her first children's book to help students learn correct letter formation and handwriting.

Dedication
Dedicated with love to my family and students.

Acknowledgment

I want to thank my husband for his unconditional love and for being my rock. My daughters for their love and the joy they have given me as their mother. My mom, papa, sisters, and brothers for all my childhood memories and adult laughs over the years. My teacher friends for our "teacher therapy" and support in keeping it all together. My wonderful mentor teacher, Dr. Maria Coady, for inspiring me to be a better teacher and complete my master's degree in education. Lastly, to all the amazing teachers who have shown me patience and kindness over the years, Thank you!

TOOLKIT BUNDLE

Check out the resources available to use with your child or students to make handwriting fun.

www.drivingletters.com

Made in the USA
Columbia, SC
11 June 2024